STUCK

OLIVER JEFFERS

HarperCollins *Children's Books*

To those who were there – Papa, Rosebud, Davebud,
the Brother, the Other Brother, Arn, Chester and San.

First published in hardback in Great Britain by HarperCollins Children's Books in 2011

10 9 8 7 6 5 4 3 2 1

ISBN: 978-0-00-726386-8

Text and illustrations copyright © Oliver Jeffers 2011

HarperCollins Children's Books is a division of HarperCollins Publishers Ltd.
The author/illustrator asserts the moral right to be identified as the author/illustrator of the work.
A CIP catalogue record for this title is available from the British Library. All rights reserved.
No part of this publication may be reproduced, stored in a retrieval system or transmitted in any form or by
any means, electronic, mechanical, photocopying, recording or otherwise, without the prior permission of
HarperCollins Publishers Ltd, 77-85 Fulham Palace Road, Hammersmith, London W6 8JB.

Visit our website at: www.harpercollins.co.uk

Printed and bound in China

IT ALL BEGAN

When Floyd got his kite stuck in A TREE.
He tried pulling and swinging but it
WOULDN'T COME UNSTUCK.

The trouble
REALLY began

when he threw his
FAVOURITE SHOE
to knock the kite loose...

...and THAT got stuck too!

He threw up his other shoe to
knock down his FAVOURITE shoe...
and, UNBELievably,
that got stuck as well.

In order to knock down
his other shoe,

Floyd fetched Mitch.

CATS get stuck in trees
all the time, but this
was GETTING RIDICULOUS.

Floyd fetched
a ladder.

He was going to sort this out
once and FOR ALL...

...and up he threw it.

I'm sure you can
guess what happened.

The ladder was borrowed
from a neighbour and
would DEFINITELY
need to be put back before
anyone noticed...

and in order to do so,
Floyd FLUNG a BUCKET of
PAINT at it.

And wouldn't you know...
the Bucket of paint got STUCK.

Then Floyd tried...

a duck to
knock down the
bucket of paint...

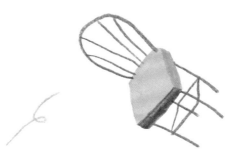

a chair
to knock down
the duck...

his friend's bicycle
to knock down
the chair...

the kitchen sink
to knock down
his friend's bicycle...

their front door to knock
down the kitchen sink...

the FAMILY car
to knock down
their front door...

the
MILKMAN
to knock down
the FAMily car...

an orang-utan to KNOCK DOWN
the milkman, who surely had
somewhere else to be...

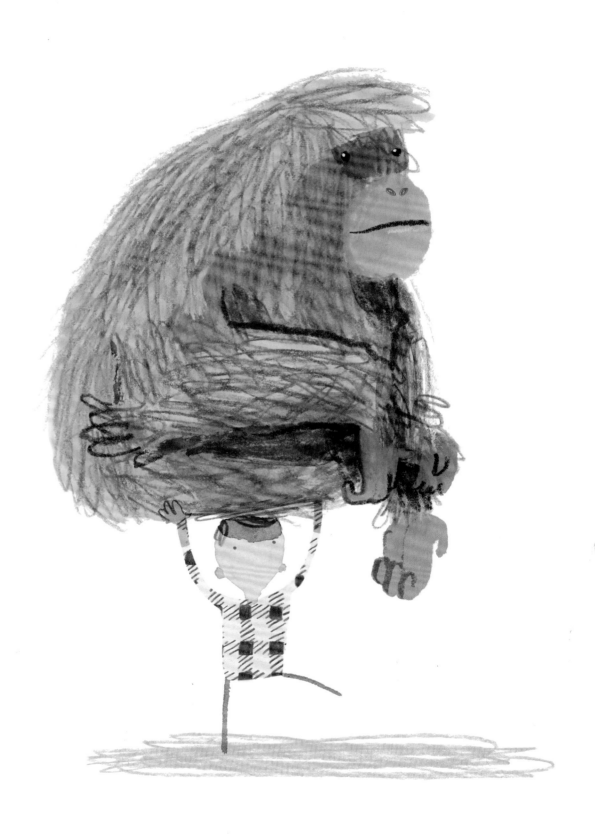

a small boat
to knock down
the orang-utan...

a BIG
BOAT
to knock
down the
small
boat...

a ~~the~~ RhinOCEROS to knock down the BIG boat...

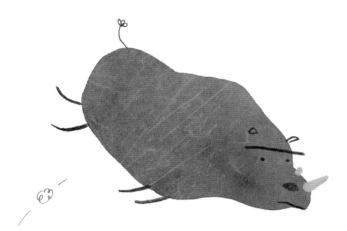

a long-distance lorry to knock down the rhinoceros...

the HOUSE across the street to knock down the long-distance lorry...

A LIGHT house to KNOCK DOWN the house no longer across the street...

a curious whale, in THE WRONG PLACE at THE WRONG TIME, to knock down the lighthouse...

and they

ALL

GOT

STUCK.

A Fire Engine was passing
and heard all the COMMOTION.
The firemen stopped to see
if they could help at all.

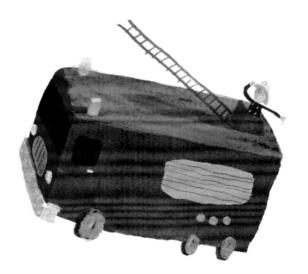

And up they went...
first the engine,

followed by the firemen, one by one.

And there they stayed,
stuck between the orang-utan
and one of the BOATS.

Firemen would DEFINITELY
be noticed missing and
Floyd KNEW he'd be in
BIG TROUBLE!

Then he had
an idea,

and went to
find a SAW.

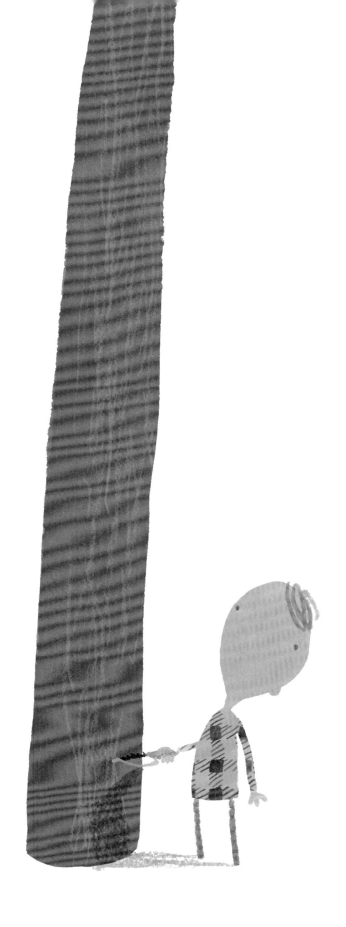

He lined it
up as best he could...

...and HURLED IT UP THE TREE.

- POP -

And that was it!
There was no more
room left in the
tree and the kite
came **unstuck**.

Floyd was delighted. He had
forgotten all about his kite
and put it to use immediately,
enjoying the rest of his DAY
very much.

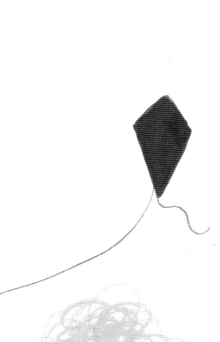

That night Floyd fell asleep exhausted.
Though before he did, he could have sworn
there was something he was Forgetting.